Don't Wait

Brennan O'Shea

Don't Wait

Acknowledgements

Some of these stories were previously published as follows:
'Field of Stones' in *Imago*, Vol. 10, No. 1, Autumn 1998;
'The Wolf and Peter' in *Goodnight Goodnight*,
Wirra Wirra Vineyards Anthology, 2009;
'Remember Me' in *Four W* Nineteen, 2008;
'Don't Wait' in *Regime* 02, March 2013;
and in *Lizard Skin Press Short Story Anthology*, Issue 2, 2014;
'Our Very Own' in *LiNQ*, Vol. 30, No. 1, May 2003;
'The Man In Green Goes To the Shire Council Offices'
in *Skive Mag*, No. 5, September 2007;
'Outside the Mirror' in *Lizard Skin Press Short Story Anthology*, Issue 1, 2012;
'The Stone-gatherer' in *Four W* Eleven, 2000.

First published 2018 by
GINNINDERRA PRESS
PO Box 3461 Port Adelaide 5015
www.ginninderrapress.com.au

Contents

Field of Stones

Finding only seagulls in the wetland area labelled 'Breeding ground for plovers' on the map, they walked on, disappointed, until they came to the cemetery.

'This is where they throw bags of cement. That's why it's called a cementery,' said Lucas.

The crows cawed in response, so Kerry did not have to laugh.

They walked round the small graveyard. Prepossessing it was not, and nowhere near old enough to be of interest to either of them. Kerry observed that one of the headstones described its owner as 'A great Unionist', an epitaph almost abusive in the current political climate. Lucas was not interested. They followed the track up to the lookout, from which the view was good, though not outstandingly so. Lucas took a few photographs then they descended and followed another track, the only other track, which led them to a field more secure than any they had seen so far. The chicken wire (heavy gauge) was taut and intact all the way round, the two rows of barbed wire above it were in perfect condition and just above waist height there was a very thick single wire which Kerry was sure was electrified.

'Just for a field of stones! And they're all wet as though someone has watered them, and not a weed in sight.'

'Stones need to be looked after, just like anything else,' Lucas replied, leaning forward to take a photograph.

There was a sharp crackling sound and he was on his knees, camera and sun hat on the ground.

'What happened?'

'I don't know. I think I had one of my blackouts.'

'Are you sure you didn't touch that electric wire and give yourself a slight shock?'

'Quite sure,' he said, replacing his sun hat and taking the photograph.

The chicken wire was now dented where Lucas had put out a hand to save himself.

Kerry was worried about 'my blackouts', occurring more frequently of late, and the occasional bed-wetting, also becoming more frequent, and the fits of absent-mindedness in which Lucas might turn a tap on and forget about it, or put the kettle on and forget it.

'A series of little strokes happening all the time,' was how the doctor had described the senile dementia which afflicted Kerry's mother, and she had forgotten taps and kettles, just like Lucas. Finally, after a power cut, they found her standing by the window, curtains still closed, striking matches because she had forgotten how to switch the torch on, and Kerry's sister Renata, a practical woman who ran a very successful nursery and garden supplies business, had insisted that their mother go into a nursing home for her own safety. She was still in the home, skin and bone, and showing no sign of recognising either of her children. Kerry feared that Lucas, years younger but looking much older than his age, was heading down the same track.

Lucas's doctor was sceptical: nothing but a bit of stress and, quite likely, a prostate problem which Lucas should have looked at. Lucas would not: other men at the over-fifties table tennis club had told him how they regretted having the prostate done (never could Kerry get a reason for this) and, in any case, he knew he did not have the problem, he just drank a lot of water. This was certainly true. Lucas would easily win the 'best flushed kidneys in South Australia' award.

The matter of declining mental powers was brushed aside. That one who had for years been the most sought after comedy scriptwriter was, at fifty-three, virtually retired and could do no better than jokes of the cementery ilk was dismissed as Kerry's imagination, natural ups and downs of such a career, and Kerry putting too much pressure on Lucas, who probably needed no more than a good holiday.

Kerry was neither convinced nor comforted but duly arranged a holiday: a birdwatching trip, this being the interest that had first brought them together. It had been pleasant enough but Lucas quite obviously no longer had the patience necessary for birdwatching. They spent most of the time walking from one likely spot to another, Lucas carelessly crashing through the landscape in a way that would frighten off any birds in the vicinity.

Strangely, he now seemed to want to be still and stay looking at the field of stones.

'What sort of stones are they?' Kerry asked, trying to break his trance-like concentration.

'I don't know. Sandstone, I suppose.'

'Not limestone?'

'Maybe. I don't know. What does it matter?' He was getting irritated.

'Time for lunch,' said Kerry briskly, 'and we need to fill the water container. You've drunk it all, and I'm quite thirsty now.'

They took a different path back, passing a tree that lay across the ground, its roots curled round a stone whose diameter was nearly a metre.

'Poor stone,' said Lucas. 'It had to push the tree over to get some air.'

They had to come back to the field of stones every morning after that, or Lucas would behave in a way that could only be described as throwing a tantrum. So Kerry indulged him. After all, why not? They were on holiday, it was an easy walk, and no hardship to look at the field of stones, always glistening as though they had just been watered. Kerry noticed that the dent in the chicken wire seemed to have been straightened out. Half an hour was long enough. Lucas was then content to leave and go wherever else Kerry might suggest.

The day they left for home, Lucas wanted to say goodbye to the stones, and wanted to go by himself. Kerry felt anxious, but agreed, and got on with the packing while he was away.

He returned an hour later, contented. 'I said goodbye to them and told them I'd come back next year. If not, they must come to collect me.'

It seemed to be a joke, so Kerry laughed.

The photograph turned out well. Lucas had it enlarged and Kerry, a silversmith, made a frame for it. Lucas approved of the metal frame, deeming it appropriate because the field had been surrounded by metal. The picture was given pride of place on the wall in the lounge and Lucas took to spending time every day just sitting looking at it.

Occasional bed-wetting continued but did not happen any more often. Sometimes Lucas would deny it, accusing Kerry of making it up; sometimes he would invent a dog in the garden or someone at the door and take the wet sheets away while Kerry was looking for the dog or the someone. Days later, Kerry would find the sheets half buried in the garden, or in a corner of the shed. It was not too big a problem to deal with: the fear of having to cope with total incontinence was far worse than the reality of washing a few extra sheets.

The turns or brainstorms were more of a worry, and were occurring more frequently. After two near accidents when Lucas was driving home from table tennis, Kerry disabled the car and had it towed away and sold, telling Lucas that the mechanic had said that it could not be repaired and (truthfully) that they could not afford to buy another. It meant no more table tennis, which made Kerry feel guilty, but Lucas did not seem very upset.

Kerry worked at making their house as safe as possible, taking over all the cooking (previously shared) and most of the housework, for fear that Lucas might electrocute or injure himself. This was in addition to taking as much work as possible to gain income. Being a few years older than Lucas, Kerry was finding life quite hard.

Renata believed that Lucas was just lazy and pretended to have brainstorms in order to get out of doing things. Having brought up five children, she considered herself expert at recognising fraud. Nevertheless, when Lucas suggested they turn their garden into a low-maintenance pebble and rock garden – no more lawnmowing and digging for Kerry – she offered to give them weed mat, stones and rocks, and calculated the quantities needed.

Lucas was disappointed with the stones and rocks; they were not what he expected, not like the stones in the field.

'Surely you wouldn't want Renata to be selling stones like those,' said Kerry, 'She just orders things in bulk to resell, and if she waters things at all, it's so they weigh more and she can make more profit.'

Lucas brightened. 'True. Perhaps if I put a few pebbles in a corner and water them and you put a silver wire fence around them, they'll grow into stones.'

Kerry laughed, for it seemed to be a joke.

Lucas had one of his turns as soon as he picked up the spade, which he dropped onto his foot, then fell on it and cut his toes. So Kerry did all the work while the injured Lucas sat inside looking at the picture. He offered to do the cooking but Kerry did not dare accept the offer. It took three days to finish the work and by then Kerry was really exhausted. Lucas ran a steaming hot bath, without letting it overflow, and Kerry gratefully soaked weary limbs and aching back while Lucas ordered a pizza so that Kerry would not have to cook or do the washing up.

Kerry slept soundly that night and dreamt of railway lines, many lines with one platform in the middle. On the platform were shoe-polishing materials, including a brand-new bright yellow duster. Kerry rebuked Lucas for his carelessness in leaving things on the platform, complaining of the cost of replacing all the things and Lucas jumped off the train to pick them up. The train started and Lucas could not catch up so Kerry jumped off too, clumsily, being weighed down by a heavy shopping bag full of fruit and vegetables, sticks of rhubarb catching in the handles of the bag…

'Wake up! Wake up! The stones are here!'

Kerry moved. The first thought that came to mind was that Lucas had wet the bed again and was trying to create a diversion, but Kerry's hand felt no dampness. This must be another brainstorm; dealing with a wet bed would have been preferable. The sound of water: Lucas was trying to fill the kettle. He would put the plug in the sink, turn on the tap and go away, leaving kettle and sink to overflow. Kerry put on the yellow towelling robe that was always ready by the bed and raced into the kitchen, getting there just in time to pull the plug and save the floor from yet another unscheduled wash.

'Put the kettle on. They're all here, every one from the field! They must have walked all night. Make some tea!'

Kerry put the kettle on. What else was there to do? This was the end. Surely the doctor would have to take notice now. Trembling with fear, tears streaming, Kerry made tea. Automatically. Then looked up as the stones came into the kitchen, all of them, just as Lucas had said.

'How can stones move so quietly?' was Kerry's last thought.

Next day, a dead man was found in the field of stones. The stones had been moved, formed into a bier, on which lay the body, aged about fifty, though could be younger, and looking serenely happy. How he came there was a mystery, for there were neither footprints nor tyre marks outside the field. He had been electrocuted, according to the autopsy report. It was said that there was not enough power in the wire to have killed him even had he wrapped in round himself many times, which, obviously, he had not done for it was intact around the field. The body was never identified.

A would-be customer found Kerry's unclothed body on the kitchen floor, appallingly bruised as if stoned to death. The yellow towelling robe was neatly folded under the head, like a pillow.

The Wolf and Peter

I knock, and listen. There is no answer, so I open the door, very slowly, and enter the room. Inside the room it is light, the curtains have been pulled back. A good sign. Peter is dressed and sitting at the table. Another good sign. Even better: the chessboard is there, ready for play.

Sometimes when I come here, the room is dark and Peter is lying in bed, face to the wall, not speaking. I have sat by the bed in silence; I have sat there talking to him; I have sat there reading to him, but whatever I do there is no response. Once, only once, I pulled the curtain back and he began to scream. Occasionally, like last week, I leave straight away. He seems not to notice.

Peter nods at me and turns his right hand upwards to indicate that I am to make the first move. This is not so good. When he is at his best, he plays a conjuring trick with acorns under egg cups to decide who shall move first. It's a simple trick, one of those that children learn first, and I could easily outwit him, but he gets such pleasure from it that I have always played along with him.

Chess is one of the bonds between us. We are equally matched, and content for a game to last through several visits. Only when he goes into one of his dark states will a cleaner insist that board and pieces be put away so that dusting can be done.

The chess set is his, carved by his grandfather, he said. Well executed cottage craftsmanship it certainly is; one can almost feel the love that went into creating each piece. The rooks are elephants, which I know to be traditional, from the Arabic, though I have not seen it before, or since. The knights are horses. The castles are towers, but each has a cat curled up on the top. The pawns are pairs of birds, different birds: I can identify ducks, swans, and a pair that might be cranes, but the others are beyond the limits of my knowledge. They are smaller birds – sparrow-shaped – though the actual pieces were made the same size as the larger birds. Is it more incongruous to see a sparrow and a crane the same size if one knows about birds than if one does not? Most interesting are the kings and queens, which are much larger than the other pieces. The red king is a huntsman, gun held ready to fire, and the red queen is a splendidly detailed wolf; the white king is an old man and the white queen a young boy. Peter says they are his grandfather and himself.

The board is mine, bought in a local shop, nothing special. Peter never mentioned his grandfather making a board to match the chess pieces, and certainly there was no board with his things when he arrived on Big Mel's doorstep one night, soaking wet, shivering, coughing badly, and moaning. It was raining that night but he was so thoroughly soaked that I am sure he had been in a creek or some other body of water for before being dumped on Mel's doorstep, and dumped there I am certain he was. His possessions were inside an Australia Post bag, the sort that mail delivery officers have, hence Mel, and then others, calling him Postman Pete. The bag was slightly damp on one side, and the things inside it, mostly clothes, were dry.

Big Mel: a hundred and eighty-five centimetres tall. A shorter woman would have been called fat but Big Mel is well proportioned, broad as well as tall. She is always called Big Mel. Her surname is Little; ludicrous to use that. Mel I assume to be short for Melanie, but I have never enquired. Big hearted she undoubtedly is, turning her ruin of a house into a refuge for elderly men found living on the streets after being liberated from mental hospitals. I'm sure the government was delighted to save money but it was a genuine theory of the time that such people should be part of the community, not kept in institutions. Many could not cope with their new, unlooked-for freedom. Mel would have taken them all in if she could. It could have been pure chance that her doorstep was chosen but I doubt it.

After half an hour, Peter says something, in Russian. I know it is Russian but I don't know what he is saying. I have forgotten my father's language. My grandfather had sense enough to leave Russia; he could see the way things were going. He settled in Italy, changing our family name to Lupo when he had learned sufficient Italian to do so. My father spoke both languages equally well but my Italian mother spoke no Russian, so it is hardly surprising that I grew up far more fluent in Italian. I can still read and speak it, despite decades of living among English speakers, and from time to time I am asked to translate.

Perhaps there is something about me that looks Russian, or what people imagine Russian should look like, for Peter does not believe that I neither speak nor understand the language, although, when he is in a good state of mind, he seems to accept my telling him so. He himself speaks English well, and with enough colloquialisms to suggest that he had been here for some years before he arrived on Big Mel's doorstep.

It was his speaking in Russian that night that prompted her to call me. Not that she could tell Russian from Italian or any other language; she knew only that it was foreign, that I am foreign and can speak foreign. Perhaps she calls me a wog. It does not matter; we respect each other for what we can do. She could not keep him because he was speaking and, delirious, shouting in Russian, and it frightened her other boarders. She would not have seven disturbed for the sake of one. So, having the authority, I arranged for him to come here. There was nothing in his post office bag to identify him, no clue to where he came from, so nowhere he could be sent back to. The government gladly accepted me as his sponsor and guarantor.

Peter's delusion is that he is Peter who caught the wolf, as in that silly children's story. No wolf could ever be caught like that, though no doubt it's comforting for children to believe it possible. He tells me the story quite often in English, and also, I believe, from the gestures he makes, in Russian. He adds details about his grandfather and the house and garden, and their life together. He does not remember his parents; they died of cholera when he was very young, he says. His grandfather kept chickens and grew vegetables; they took walks together in the forest, gathering mushrooms, and berries in summer. There was a huntsman who came to visit sometimes, bringing a hare or duck that he had shot, and talking late into the night with the grandfather. All, or any, of these things could be true. Or not.

I played him Prokofiev's music once, without narration, and he went to sleep. I tried again and he was fidgety, obviously bored, giving no sign of recognition. He says he does not like music, and that seems to be true. He has a radio set, but does not use it often; I'm told that he listens to a horse racing station when he does have it on. Once, I played him a record of Russian folk songs and he seemed bored by that too, and told me to 'stop that noise'.

I could not find a Russian language record of *Peter and the Wolf* so I had to play it in English, an old version narrated by Boris Karloff.

'It's your story, Peter. Don't you remember it?'

'No. What about the *kasha* we had for breakfast? And my new shoes that I had to keep clean? That's why I was supposed to stay in the garden. The end is wrong: I let the wolf go and he became a friend for me to play with. Wolves are like that, you know.'

Kasha he'd spoken of before but the story about the shoes was new, and I have not heard it again, nor that he released the wolf, though he had, occasionally, mentioned a wolf playmate.

Twice more I tried to play the record but he became irritated. 'I don't want to hear that. Because it's wrong.' And he threw himself onto his bed, face to the wall, fingers blocking his ears, and refused to speak to me.

Today, after another half-hour, I am near to having him in check.

He says, 'Let's go to the garden. I'll show you the tree where I tied up the wolf.'

This will not break my concentration: as he well knows, I can wait for as long as need be for him to decide his next move. It's a pleasant, warm summer day so why not go down to the garden? It's a welcome lightening of his mood.

The large old plane tree is at its best in late summer, giving shade; and magnificent in autumn when the leaves change colour. I cannot quite credit plane trees in a Russian forest but what do I know? If Peter believes that it was a tree like this where he caught the wolf…well, so be it. We sit on the bench under the tree looking across the garden to the fountain behind the roses. Peter takes his sun hat off and puts it on the bench beside me. He is bald, and always conscientious about protecting his head from the sun. Here, in the shade of the tree, he is quite safe.

'I can't climb trees now. You feed me too well!' He laughs heartily.

I smile, and nod. True, he is weightier now than when he came here; not obese, just slightly rotund. It suits him; he looks younger. I believe in feeding patients good meals. Big Mel and I agree that good food leads to contentment, giving reason to stay; and of those few who do run away, most come back at dinner time. Peter has never tried to run away. This is his home now, and he knows he belongs to me. We shall play chess and walk in the garden until one of us dies.

Peter stands, walks behind the bench, and puts the noose around my neck. I am surprised by the speed and dexterity with which he does this.

'This is how I caught the wolf. We both know this is how to do it. Not like your stupid story. Move and you will choke. Right?'

I nod, and smile. This is not something he has done before. Where he found the curtain cord I do not know. In his right hand, he holds the weight.

'I will throw it,' he shouts, 'up into the tree.' He does so. 'And when I catch it, I will string you up. Like an American cowboy. They have wolves in America too. They know how to catch wolves. Not by the tail!' He stands there, looking up into the tree where the weight has been caught in the leaf-laden branches. 'By the tail! Hah! You don't have a tail!'

I remove the cord around my neck, and loosen the hair pins to free my long grey hair which I wind around my hand and push through the noose. 'Yes I do, Peter. Here. Catch me by my tail.'

He whirls round. 'She wolf!' he shrieks, hysterically. 'She wolf!' and starts to cry.

As I take his arm to guide him back inside, the gardener approaches from behind the tree.

'Oh. Dr Lupo. Well, you seem to have everything under control…'

'Yes. Thank you. Please try to remove this cord without damaging the tree. Then take it to the housekeeper. We must find out where he got it.'

'She wolf, she wolf.' Peter sobs.

No one takes any notice. He is obviously under control. I put his sun hat back on his head and lead him back to his room.

Remember Me

Fernie had dozed off while watching the cricket match. I was reading. I turned the sound down. It was still loud enough for the commentary to be heard, should Fernie wake, but less intrusive. I would not be disturbed if someone hit a six or was controversially out. I could hear the birds now, those birds I always hear on summer nights, never in the daytime; definitely not nightingales but I don't know what they are. It's a short, two-note, mid-pitch call that's repeated over and over yet never seems jarring or repetitive. I like to hear it. I find it a comforting sound.

I did not hear Death come in. As one doesn't. He sat in the third armchair. The only vacant one in the room, diagonally opposite Fernie, slanted away from the television set and slightly towards me, though not face to face.

I say 'he' because he was dressed in a man's suit, dark navy, with socks to match, black lace-up shoes and a blue pinstripe shirt, open at the neck. No tie. I've met Death several times before, usually wearing jeans – designer jeans – and T-shirt with monogrammed pocket – MM in antique script – and expensive-looking footwear. Never, never in grim reaper garb.

'Why ever would I dress like that? I'm trying not to frighten people!' s/he told me once. 'It's insulting. I should sue them!'

On that occasion, Death was dressed as a woman, in a lime-green business suit and white shirt, and carrying a document bag which looked as though it contained a laptop computer.

The only other time I saw Death dressed as a woman she wore a flowing red silk dress and had shoulder-length blonde ringlets that bounced around her face as she walked through the art gallery in hand-crafted leather sandals.

He had blond curly hair that evening too, but much shorter, rather too short for the round cherubic face.

'No one is ever ready,' he said, seeming to answer me, though I had said nothing, had hardly even thought. 'Least of all most of those who say they are, and even some who call for me. They're daring themselves, like children who jump into the swimming pool because they're frightened of others seeing how frightened they are. I could make it so much easier if only they would look into themselves.'

I looked across at Fernie, and tears came. After so long, after so much, for either one of us to be left seemed unbearable. Yet I knew, of course, that it must be that way.

Death knelt beside me, patting my arm, and gave me the neatly folded handkerchief from the top pocket of his jacket. 'No, no. Not either of you. Not this time.'

I could not feel the slightly translucent fingers patting my arm but sensed the comfort coming through,

'Not this time,' he repeated. 'Not yet. Think of this as a social call.'

'Should I offer you a cup of tea then?' I said, drying my eyes on the fine white linen handkerchief monogrammed MM in blue, in antique script, in one corner.

Death laughed heartily and settled back into the chair. 'We'll meet many times before you come with me. Either of you. When it's time, I'll accept the return of my handkerchief. Remember that.' Then he left.

He took my granddaughter that night. I'll never forgive him for that. Or the years since, in the cancer ward, where Fernie and I seem to alternate, each time for longer, and in greater pain, and each less able to care for the other when we are home together. Most of all, I'll never forgive Death for the love turning to loathing as we wait to qualify for the special hell of High Level Care.

I have met Death many times since that evening. The handkerchief was always with me, carried in the hope that I might return it.

Always it was refused, with a smile and a whispered, 'Not yet. Not this time.'

Once, furious after rejection, I tried to burn it. Another time, I cut it into tiny pieces and soaked the pieces in caustic soda. Both times, it was there again next day, that fine white linen handkerchief monogrammed MM in blue, in antique script, in one corner.

Death was dressed as a priest when I last met him, a modern, young priest in street clothes: chinos and a light grey shirt with dark blue crosses embroidered on the corners of its collar. No tie, but with a gilt crucifix, rather too large, I thought, hanging round his neck. I looked him in the eyes but he turned away, into a butcher's shop. I followed, slowly, in pain.

There were no other customers in the shop and the butcher was wrapping some meat as I limped in. He blessed the butcher.

I hit him in the face with my walking stick and hissed, 'Remember me, Death!'

'Memento mori,' he replied, in that soothing, clerical tone of total indifference to the sufferings of others. Then, 'Bless you, my child.'

I was so angry I picked up the cleaver from the counter and killed him.

No one can kill Death. I had murdered a real priest.

The defence lawyer tried to find excuses for me, but I had seen my way out. I could not afford to be judged insane, so I expressed my hatred of all religion very coolly and carefully, making it clear that I would dearly like to kill other members of the clergy and would take any chance I had to do so. My sentence, with all possible remission, is far longer than I can possibly live. I shall make certain that I never qualify for any parole.

The handkerchief was taken away from me, with other personal possessions. I cannot have it in prison. No one can bring it to me. Except Death. And if Death returns it to Death, then I shall not have done so. In a way, I'll be cheating Death.

I like that idea.

Ethel Merman Will Not Remember

Enjoy the legend, as I do: it is neat, tidy, rather charming even.

But they got it wrong. They made it wrong: they had to have a happy ending, a right ending. Which meant their perception of a right, and therefore happy, ending when the erring woman finally saw the light and accepted the fate of a person of faith. Christian faith of course, perhaps others faiths too, Buddhism excepted. The light of death: the light that goes out at the end of the tunnel. That was what they offered and, I suppose, believed in.

My happy ending is a new life: rebirth, rising again, if you will, but on this earth, in this dimension. That is what I really chose. I left as soon as I had the envelope. Poor old Prus, as the playwright named him, was snoring his head off; a little something in the wine saw to that.

I went to my mother's people, the Roma, whose knowledge my father used when developing the formula. Locating the document was not quite as described in the play but had been difficult enough and I was determined not to be in that situation again, so I apprenticed myself to the Healer and learned how to prepare the tincture myself. I learnt many other things too, far more complex than my little formula. I'll never understand why the Healer did not use it herself; something to do with obedience to the Nature Goddess she served. Religion and I just do not seem able to get along together. I could have taken her place but it was not the standard of living I was used to. Luxury and I certainly do get along very well! And Art: singing gypsy songs at village fairs does not compare with opera.

Moving on turned out to be a very wise choice: events in Europe at that time were growing sinister, though I admit I did not foresee any more than anyone else, despite my Roma origins. I began again in a provincial town but was soon offered roles in a more prestigious company and touring several capitals. I was advised to leave. Switzerland was quite popular and one could easily cross the border on foot, I was told. True, no doubt, but not an option I fancied. America was the refuge of choice for me.

It was, and still is, hard for me to see what was happening in Europe at that time as real, and not just another opera plot. Am I deficient in feeling for my fellow humans? Selfish? Perhaps. Once I had acquired false papers, I played the Diva to get to the front of the queue for a passage; and then for the best accommodation and attention on the boat. I sang, occasionally, and only for those who might have influence. Not to cast pearls before swine: that relic of the Christian faith has become a guiding precept, as the old Priest would say.

America, specifically Hollywood, was amazing. I thrived. Dancing came easily: I have good coordination and the legs for it, so opera, movies, musicals were all open to me. I chose carefully. I became moderately wealthy, moderately famous, for now I knew the value of anonymity for one who has to disappear then reappear as another. A few interviews, a few articles, no books, definitely no biographies; any difficult questions and this Diva would sweep out. That did me no lasting harm. There was always another, less temperamental but less interesting and far less talented, so, in time, they came back to me.

The actress in me enjoys learning new roles. When it comes to the wisdom of maturity, I have centuries of it to draw on.

One changes mentally as much as physically over a lifetime, outgrowing friends. Yes, I recall them with affection, great affection for some, but my mind outgrew them, reached out to new friends. I chose to go before love soured, while still holding them in that affection.

I was sad the first time, because I had not made the choice myself, it was imposed, and I harboured bitterness. It took half another lifetime for me to forgive, as the Priest would have said, but I prefer the twentieth century term 'let go'. Now I look forward to my new beginnings.

Perhaps I'll even forget Sean, the Irish psychologist with the most beautiful long red hair curling over freckled shoulders; he was an experience I would not want to have missed, for the peace of the grave! Never! I am blessed, not cursed. Sean explained to me what I had done, though he never knew, of course, what he was doing. He thought he was telling me his own story, how he himself had accepted becoming paraplegic after diving into shallow water. All his own fault, he said, smiling, but he had moved on (a popular phrase of that time) and made a new life for himself through helping others.

All that beautiful red hair and those freckled shoulders…

'Difficult but not impossible,' he said.

I was afraid of complications, of disappointment, and said so.

He laughed heartily and kissed my hand.

No such problems with the Zen master in the mountains. That three months I spent in the monastery is another experience I would not want to have missed. I went there so that I could disappear and re-emerge unnoticed. I told him my story knowing it would not impress him, blurring states of consciousness being commonplace in that environment. He did not want me to take the dose, not because he wanted me to accept death, which hardly exists in his philosophy, but he thought I should move into my next phase by using my mind, as in Zen meditation, not through chemical aid.

I could have stayed there indefinitely, working at the meditation, but when he told me it could take several lifetimes to reach the state of Zen rebirth, it sounded somewhat like the salvation stories the Christians preached at me centuries ago. Besides, I had made arrangements for my next life and was really looking forward to it. So I took the dose that night and left in the morning for Australia.

Australia, and a pharmacy degree. Becoming a student, adding science to my Roma knowledge. It was an extraordinary experience for me who had not even attended school (my father educated me), though perhaps that was an advantage: less to unlearn, no resentment over past humiliation. I really enjoyed my student days and I was given so much help by a wonderful librarian that I graduated with the highest marks ever. Having a plan in mind, I next enrolled in a marketing course. Leo really approved of that and gave even more help. He taught me to drive too, and arranged for me to buy a car from a friend of his. He loved jazz, so often took me to the jazz club where he played saxophone, and encouraged me to sing there.

There is always a connecting thread, both in a current life and between one life and another. My lovely librarian did not really like the American 1930s-era jazz that I knew so well from my past, but there were other, more academic musicians who did. Leo went to India, for the dusky maidens, and, I suspect, the odd puff of drugs. I went to the country, to the foothills of the Snowy Mountains, with an ageing New Age academic to meet his Zen master who was, as I had guessed, my old friend. He looked very, very old indeed, as of course he is, and though he had no illness he was becoming feeble, as the old do. He told me was looking forward to his next life on a higher plane. That is the difference between us: I want my next lives in this dimension. He told me he felt like that for the first hundred years or so, and that, eventually, I, too, will seek a higher plane. I doubt it, but did not dispute it. We are both planning for the future in the light of how we feel in the present. He offered refuge at any time I might need it.

I returned with my academic: to sing jazz for him, and to borrow money from him to set up my natural health pharmacy. It was the time for such enterprises and it did very well. I was soon able to move the dispensing side of the business to the monastery, training some of the novices to assist me. They learned quickly; most were keen to move on to higher things but two decided to remain with me, and another, disenchanted with monastery life, asked to work for me in the retail establishment. I told him he must first grow his hair; smooth bald heads became fashionable later but at that time it was long locks for romantic appeal. Romantic appeal sells products; and tickets to the opera.

Opera is the one thing I always want to return to. My academic introduced me to his brother, a retired law professor who was, he said, a good contact. I went to his tenth-floor apartment overlooking the harbour and sang for him. He recognised my genius of course but was not encouraging about my career prospects. He described the long, dreary route through the conservatorium system; he suggested it might be wise for me to go to Europe, where fame would certainly come more quickly and I might be invited to return to Australia to sing. It was not an appealing option but I was considering it when he sat up, clapped his hands and announced that there was another way, a way I might go straight to the top. He told me.

I was appalled; appalled and insulted. 'How dare you! How dare you!' I shrieked at him, and started smashing a set of oriental-looking vases until I was grasped and pushed against the wall with a hand across my throat.

'Who do you think you are, madam! You're a middle-aged chemist, that's all, a chemist with a good voice but no background. Have you a past reputation? Have you?'

That stopped me. I almost heard my Zen master warning me, solemnly, that to slip into behaviour from a past life is to endanger the future.

The law professor continued, 'You've smashed a valuable vase in your silly childish tantrum. Irreplaceable. I can sue you, ruin you, unless you do as I say. And you will win. You cannot fail.'

He was right.

Jumping through the hoops of Operatunity Oz was definitely degrading, I shall always feel that, though it was mildly amusing to act the part of a naive wannabe, as the law professor called me. Naturally, I won. Financially too: he placed bets for both of us. I have never placed a bet in any of my lives but it seems that Australian academics routinely do so.

It led me to the stage of the Sydney Opera House, taking curtain calls after the final performance, receiving bouquets, and savouring every microsecond of it. The reviews were ecstatic: 'the greatest Makropoulos ever'. Well, of course.

I toured Europe, then the USA, by invitation, singing only in the great opera houses, with the then world's most renowned conductors, tenors, orchestras and opera companies, all of them clamouring to perform with me.

The best is yet to come. What will it be? To sing Rusalka's song to the moon in an opera house on the moon? Perhaps, in passing, on the way to the outer galaxies. It will happen, in one of my future lives. I may become the Diva of Alpha Centauri…or…? How could I – how could anyone – not want such a glorious, exciting future?

As for that nonsense about the initials, it was the playwright's invention, a literary conceit, nothing more. There is no reason at all why I should keep the same ones, and I have not. I was never Ethel Merman. My voice and legs will always be far better than hers ever were.

Don't Wait

Propaganda is a wonderful thing. Some of us ignore it, always. Some of us eventually succumb and adopt the right opinion. Some of us leap onto it with enthusiasm…

My sister Ellie for one: real name Joy, or was it Joyce? We were born on the same day and even at the same time, allegedly, but to different mothers; presumably we had different fathers. I've never bothered to find out; I feel no need to know. I am free to be as I choose without either blaming my forebears or having to give them all the credit.

We were adopted by a couple who liked the idea of having disconnected twins and the chance it gave to prove that astrology is rubbish. They had several birth charts prepared for us by reputed astrologers and bound into books. I keep mine because it's the only thing I have from them: they were killed in a car crash when we were about two and a half.

We grew up by the beach, brought up by Gran, our adopting mother's mother. Gran had either been a teacher or wanted to be one, I forget which, and read to us the stories she called classics and from one of these – the *Water Babies*, I think – she took the name Ellie and applied it to my sister, who loved both beach and sea so much. My sister loved the name Ellie and always used it from then on, hence my forgetting her original name.

Ellie had long, curly, fair hair – golden, Gran called it – and blue eyes and was thought pretty as a child, beautiful as a woman. She was always good-natured, obedient, kind…too good to be true, but she was true. She was my sister and everyone loved her.

Those were the days when we were encouraged to respect old people. The local MP's newsletter always pictured him with old people, at a club or new retirement facility praising their achievements, congratulating those who had lived a hundred years, stayed married for fifty years, and so on. Local newspapers had more of the same. The words 'elders' and 'seniors' were almost obligatory; no one dared say, or write, 'old people'. I'm sure there was even a senior of the year, a ninety-year-old who had gained a Master of Medicine degree, or climbed Everest with a crocodile… Stupid waste of time and effort, I thought, but Ellie was full of admiration. She wrote a composition about our wonderful grandmother who looked after us and won the Principal's Special Prize for it, a special prize, for she was only ever near top of the lower half of the class. I bust the nose of the only one who dared to say dumb blonde but no matter how hard she worked, Ellie was never going to be an English teacher for Gran.

A friend of Gran's took Ellie into her hairdressing business, where she worked even harder and really seemed to have a talent for it. She left to look after Gran, nursing her through Alzheimer's for years, and then cancer. I stayed away, moving around, both here and overseas, as geologists do, and was overseas when Gran died. Ellie sent me a copy of a memoir of Gran that appeared in the local newspaper; the last few lines commended Ellie for her loving care of Gran. It took up two columns of the top half of the page. The third column had part of an article about elders being a drain on the social purse, making life harder for the young who had to pay crippling taxes to support these people and their expensive health care.

When I came back, two years later, Ellie had returned to hairdressing. She was still living in Gran's house; fine by me. I like the beach, but prefer the hills and solitary bush walks, so I bought an isolated cottage as a base camp, intending to move further out and build my own place when I retired, which I did in my fifties. We lived separate lives, but always met for lunch – celebration was Ellie's word, though I didn't see it that way – on our shared birthday.

On the birthday when I reached official retirement age, there were two letters in the box: one was a very large envelope, almost certainly the usual effusive card from Ellie, and an official letter:

Your government commends you for your contribution to society through your past years of employment but regrets that you feel unable to continue in employment. Many citizens find it fulfilling to continue working until their mid-seventies or even longer.

However, it is noted that you have secured adequate financial support and will not be applying for the Government Aid for Elderly Citizens' Allowance (formerly known as Age Pension).

Your government hopes that you will continue to serve the community in a voluntary capacity.

This letter is to inform you that you must register with GovVolLink for assistance in finding Approved Community Service Employment and to obtain your Community Servant Transport Card which entitles you to free public transport to and from your Approved Community Service Employment.

Your government is determined to prevent the exploitation of volunteers that has occurred in the past and, in particular, to ensure that all Occupational Health and Safety regulations are complied with so it is now illegal to undertake any Community Service Employment without GovVolLink approval. If you have commenced working in any sort of voluntary capacity, you must register with GovVolLink within two weeks of receiving this letter.

Your government wishes you the best of health.

Unfortunately some older citizens suffer from extremely painful and debilitating problems so, in the cause of alleviating human misery your government has arranged for all senior citizens to receive the Government Compassion Package. This should arrive within two weeks of this letter. Should this not occur, please contact my department.

Jocelyn Smith
Seniors Consultant Specialist
Ministry of Human Services

Sod that for a lark! I thought. What kind of no-hoper has to work for nothing? Besides, I'd earned my retirement and I intended to enjoy it. I threw the letter into the bin.

One of the small pleasures of retirement is getting up when one wakes, no more bullying by an alarm clock, and I was at risk of being late. That day was bright and sunny, warm for the time of year, perfect for lunch by the beach, but it was an hour's drive to get to Kafe Athene, Ellie's favourite place.

Every station I tuned to seemed to have a talkback program with someone complaining about the high taxes we paid because so much was spent on the selfish oldies…definitely not what I wanted to hear. Finally I found a station playing the most extraordinary jazz version of Beethoven's Fifth that I have ever heard. It was one of those volunteer-run community stations and I was about to ring them for details of the CD when I noticed that I was right behind a police car.

As I said, I'd earned my retirement and I meant to enjoy it. And I did: building my own house and travelling, mostly overseas but back here in later years when the be-patriotic-and-holiday-at-home advertisements had ceased; and, to be truthful, I was tired of long flights. After the last such trip, I spent two weeks eating and sleeping and sorting through mail, throwing ninety per cent of it away. Another official letter, about six months old, was there:

This letter is to inform you that legislation is now in force requiring all citizens over the age of 17 and not in paid employment to contribute a minimum of two years Approved Community Service Employment to society.

According to GovVolLink records, you have not taken part in any Approved Community Service Employment.

As you reached age 70 just before legislation was passed, you are exempt but your government would like to encourage you to take part in Service to the Community. You will surely find it most fulfilling, as so many other citizens have, and a great way to enjoy the company of your fellow citizens.

Please be aware that any sort of voluntary work, even looking after sick or disabled family members, must be registered with GovVolLink for assessment as Approved Community Service Employment.

Your government gives formal acknowledgement to contributing citizens by funding Local Government Community Service Employment morning tea ceremonies at which Volunteer of the Year certificates in various categories are awarded.

Please note that the Government Compassion Package sent to you five years ago has been superseded.

Your updated Government Compassion Package will be sent to you in the next two weeks. Should this not occur, please contact me at the address/phone number/email address at the top of this letter.

Your GP can assist you if you have any difficulty understanding the instructions.

Jocelyn Smith
Seniors Consultant Specialist
Ministry of Human Services

No sign of any package in the pile of mail; perhaps because no one was there to sign for it. I had not seen Ellie for a couple of years; I wondered what effect that letter had had on her. Deliberately, I had not contacted her for our recent birthday celebration; I regretted that now. She had been working at two jobs when I left, anxious not to be a burden on the young, determined to look after herself,

'I'm going to do what it says in the National Seniors' Advice. It's from the government, not a paper or magazine or on television, so don't tell me it's all rubbish!' she had said. She stopped short of telling me how selfish I am.

We agreed to meet for lunch the next day, not at Kafe Athene but at a pub some streets away and not overlooking the beach. It was a pub that offered pensioner meals; nothing fancy but reasonable quality at a reasonable price in a clean, light dining room, handy for the pokies. It was close to one of the three high-level care facilities where she now worked as a volunteer. One of her employers had sacked her because she looked old – 'not a good advertisement for the salon' – and when a friend showed her an article about selfish oldies keeping young people out of paid work by hanging on too long, Ellie had decided to leave the other job. She sold Gran's house and invested the money as advised by a government financial advisor so that she had an income and even though she qualified, she had managed, so far, not to apply for the Government Aid for Elderly Citizens.

'I'm so happy. It really is fulfilling, you know!' and she did, indeed, look happy; if tired. Not old, though; Ellie always looked young.

Too late to challenge the sacking now, even if she would let me. I felt angry, but managed to say nothing.

'I have a late birthday present for you.' She gave me a suitcase containing things from Gran's house that she thought I might like to have.

> Congratulations on being one of the first recipients of the new GovCares Kit. This replaces the former Australian Government Compassion Package.
>
> If you have any difficulty at all in understanding the instructions, you should contact your GP, who, thanks to recently passed amendments to Equal Opportunity legislation, is legally obliged to assist you in the use of the GovCares Kit.
>
> Alternatively, as you are now 75, you can access assistance and counselling from the newly established Assistance to Venerable Australians wing of the Department of Human Services.
>
> Argyle Zatopek
> Minister for Human Services

That one was waiting for me when I came back from a two-year-long camping trip on which, deliberately, I had kept away even from very small towns. My success in being self-sufficient while travelling was gratifying; now I intended to live that way at home. I hoped Ellie would join me. I began work on a speech, something about ending our lives together as we had begun them. Sickening, but only sentimental slush like that would have a chance of persuading her.

The next day's mail had an invitation to the Shining Example. The state governor, federal government ministers, the state premier, and various others would be in attendance; and my sister would be in the leading role. For the first time in her life. I know I should have been there too, but I couldn't, I just couldn't support what she was doing.

I went back to the pub where we'd last met for lunch. It had changed, as things do, as things should. The dining room had become a sort of local sports museum: photos, trophies, records of scores in games over twenty years and suchlike had replaced the rural prints and vases of flowers. There were even more TV screens showing different sports programs. I looked around, glancing at the staff: they all seemed to be new, no one to recognise me. My guess that the corner screen would still show national interest news items was correct.

I bought a beer, took it to a table in a corner where the screen could be viewed without, I hoped, anyone viewing me. I couldn't hear everything too well because of the general noise level in the bar but that didn't matter. I didn't want to hear all the political speeches; I really didn't want to hear my sister. I feared I would succumb to reading the captions. I was right about that.

First, of course, the National Anthem, then speeches, all praising the unavoidably absent Argyle Zatopek, the architect of the scheme, for his foresight: such ingenuity and such humanity. Of course! No such person; a committee – has to be. He was next praised for his brilliance in composing the scheme's anthem – 'Don't wait to be told / You don't need to grow old' then sung by a choir – almost – but cut off for advertisements. The program came back just in time for the procession.

So there she was, in a long, flowing white robe with her long, flowing white hair floating out behind her as she walked – floated almost – along a white carpet. She carried a bunch of white lilies, holding it, very tightly, with both hands. The reporter said she looked angelic – I bet that was scripted for him – and described the expression on her face as seraphic. I'd have said soppy. He went on about the vision in white leading the procession. She was followed by three groups of relatives, looking grim, some weeping, and each carrying a picture of one of the examples from the high-level care facilities where Ellie worked. Every example was inspired by Ellie, according to the commentator. That, I could understand. In such a state of health, having to endure life in such places…why not? Next was a shot of the examples: all in white, each with a lily, and with an attendant standing by. Only Ellie had been alone.

The program was interrupted for an important horse race. A caption said they would come back to it but I felt sick already. I left. I walked along the street wondering how such a shy nervous person as my sister could be part of such a show. It occurred to me later that she might have been drugged. I hope she was.

There are pictures of Ellie in every suburb or small town now. She has become a sort of saint: there are Shining Example ceremonies every month and a special one commemorating her every year, on our birthday. I avoid them.

I'm ninety-three today. No letter from the government this time. They can't find me. I'm sure of that. I'm a permanent camper now and probably the oldest person in the country. It can't last of course. Not that I want to make the ton, but I am determined to die of natural causes.

And to hell with their blasted GovCares Kit.

Our Very Own

The first day was towards the end of winter, the time of year when it can be so cold and bleak that it can only be sheer insanity that leads retailers to fill their shops with summer clothes; or so mild and balmy that it takes great self-discipline to resist the temptation to wash jumpers and socks and put them away instead of wearing them. It was a day of the latter type towards the end of a week of being not so warm as it looks, the cold still biting at the first and last of the day. It was just a slight mist, of the wispy white floating variety beloved by nature poets, a morning mist that stayed all day. Across to the hills it was grey, blurred as if storm and rain were brewing. Across to the sea likewise, the horizon fuzzy.

On the beach itself, the atmosphere was clammy, the mist a little more obvious than in the street, yet the sun burned and the icy wind that whipped through the unprotected Eustachian passages did not lift the slightly damp sand. Dolphins were diving for fish, a pair of pelicans skimmed along the tideline, among the gulls a pair of young kelp gulls, not previously seen this far north, were a sight for comment. There may have been the usual boats on the furry grey horizon.

'You need glasses,' said an elderly neighbour, 'And those special irises of yours need water. Look how they're drying out. Got to look after the Lunchtime Lovers. Attend to the earache first, though. Nasty thing, earache.'

A week later: on the beach again, ears protected this time, eyes tested and vision pronounced perfect, the horizon was still fuzzy, hiding small boats, though not the tanker proceeding to the refinery. The mist might have been a little thicker, a little damper; the sun still burned and the wind now did raise the sand a little, sticking it to below-knee clothing moistened by mist, but it was a land wind only; the waves lapped gently at the edge of the millpond sea.

Another week, and the patches of mist floating slowly through the streets had thickened. The airport was closed. Someone rang a talkback radio programme to ask why the wind had not blown the mist away, and a coarse joke was the reply, starting a debate about ethics and courtesy of talkback show hosts which dominated all the commercial stations, the press, and even the national broadcaster. After a fortnight, the various unions and managements issued a joint statement which blithered about courtesy but said, in essence, that when one of the lunatic fringe raised a silly issue, any sort of dismissal was justified, even commendable. Astoundingly, the statement was endorsed by the Attorney-General. Not long after that, the weather forecasts stopped. People no longer talked about the weather, pretending that the mist was not there, or, conversely, that it had always been there exactly as it was at any given second of awareness.

In time, the separate clouds of mist became one mass, not moving but thickening, through which the sun burnt and the wind blew. The airport was closed down, a fact not reported, but no one could book a flight out or in; travel agents went out of business. The elderly neighbour's air traffic controller daughter packed her family into the car and possessions onto the newly acquired trailer, saying she had been transferred interstate. She begged her father to go with them but he refused, saying he was too old to move. Tears streaming, she drove away, leaving her house unsold and untenanted. He said then that he had stayed to keep her out of trouble; she had had to sign an oath of secrecy and it would have looked suspicious if he had gone too. He was not believed.

The sight of the hills around the city became a memory, though it was still possible to drive there, slowly, with lights on. On the beach, it was possible to see the waves gently flowing, more like river water, into the thick wall of seaweed at the water's edge. But no further. The crunching, squelching sound of walking on weed was absorbed by the mist; seagulls appeared silently, then disappeared; there seemed to be more kelp gulls. The cold wet sand behind the seaweed was gathered by the wind and flung, stinging the face, clinging to clothes. Plodding through the warm weed was preferable. Warm, because the sun still burned. At night, the weed was cold, crackling, frosty, lit by minute blue flashes from gem-like organisms momentarily catching light. Light. From the unseen moon?

The elderly neighbour offered his collection of football scarves to wrap round the irises: the thick wool would keep them at an even temperature and absorb moisture so they would not dry out, he said.

There was another major earthquake, this time in Africa. A letter appeared in the paper about the violence of man being reflected in the violence of nature. This was denounced as blasphemy by a government minister. The archbishop issued a statement, incomprehensible bar the last sentence urging the faithful to contribute to the appeal for the victims, which the religious took as endorsement of the government minister and they resolved to be positive, pray harder and contribute. The irreligious saw the archbishop as trying to undermine the government; comments were made about a stupid old fart who should be ignored since he couldn't be shot.

When it became impossible to see across the road, the street lights were left on all day and turned off at night. The speed limit was lowered and drivers were ordered to keep lights on at all times. People were advised to put reflector lights on fences, gates, doors. They did, but there was no light to be reflected. Everyone owned at least one powerful torch, and batteries were rationed. Not that it was dark; it was just thick white mist at all times, bright like snow when the sun no one could see was shining, and dull white when it was not. Thick, damp and quiet. No one complained about noise any more. Jet engines roaring in and out of the airport would not have been heard. And there were a few government flights. Or so it was reported on a community radio station that lost its licence within days of the broadcast. But news can never be stopped; word always gets through somehow.

The government tried to discourage use of the internet: grave psychological damage was inevitable, treatment costing millions to the grossly overburdened mental health department. Net searchers were likened to drug addicts, to be helped, to be pitied, to be cured. It was reasonably successful: the law-abiding desisted; those who continued became very discreet. News still got around. News that interstate bus and train services had been cancelled at the request of the state government. News that local train services would be next; this despite the fact that the trains were still running on time.

The beach was a whirling blizzard; it was impossible to get through to the seaweed at the water's edge, if indeed the seaweed was still there.

'Get yourself a suit of armour,' said the elderly neighbour, 'like Ned Kelly's. Felt those irises lately? The early ones should be out any day. Better protect them from the wind, though. You don't want the Affaires broken off!'

Yet life went on. People still went to work, to school, to shop, to worship, to entertainment on weekends. It was amazing how little had changed rather than how much. The human organism had shown how well it could adapt to change. The slowing of transport had lengthened the working day considerably, so people stayed home in the evenings. The hills became almost another country. People stayed in their home suburbs because to venture further was a major expedition. But this was not a return to the village life of the past; there was no sense of local community. The phones still worked, and television and video became even more central to people's lives, albeit with locally made news bulletins only, as the mist blocked anything from interstate. Or so it was said.

The Health Commission recommended viewing in a completely dark room: no danger to eyesight at all and it would conserve power. The health risks were still obesity, raised cholesterol, skin cancer and certain transmissible diseases. The road toll was at the same level but poor visibility was the risk factor rather than speed; injuries, however, were generally less serious with everyone driving so slowly. A benefit of the mist. There had been no adverse effect on health, even among the aged.

Rumour said otherwise. Rumour said one in five houses was empty because elderly occupants were dying of pneumonia. Rumour said, too, that the mist was a government experiment, pumped in from the sea to the city and suburbs; that in the hills there was no mist, that people there still lived the way they always had, that the government had sealed the city electronically so that no one could drive to the hills, let alone interstate.

Urban myth said people were digging tunnels through to the hills.

An editorial appeared deploring the spreading of rumours that created alarm and despondency and lack of confidence in the government.

A caller to talkback radio likened the mist to the smog of London in the fifties.

'Nonsense!' said the elderly neighbour, a migrant who had lived in London during the smog years. 'Our mist is friendly. A white fluffy blanket keeping us safe, not a sulphurous stink causing horrible respiratory problems.'

The word 'fog' was never used. No advice, no decree, yet everyone knew that it was a forbidden word.

Another big earthquake, this time in India, and several small ones interstate, but it couldn't happen here, said a government minister; our mist protected us by releasing the pressures that caused earthquakes.

'Makes it sound like hellfire getting out,' said the elderly neighbour, 'except it's too cold. He needs a new speech writer. Any sign of the Blackouts yet?'

The police commissioner announced a big drop in property crime statistics: 'Our very own mist has made this the safest state to live in.'

Urban myth said gangs of blind burglars had raised the level of property crime to an all-time high.

The elderly neighbour invited everyone in the street, a crescent of twenty houses, to a party at noon on Sunday. Five people came and were served champagne and caviar.

'Let us drink to our very own mist. It is a year ago this very day that we all pretended not to notice the very first wisp of what was the good life to come!'

There was much disagreement about the date, but none about the beneficial effect of the mist. More champagne, and there were some complaints about the wind.

'But don't you see, we need the wind to keep the mist out of the houses!' He opened all the windows and both doors, and the mist stopped on the threshold as if blocked by an invisible screen.

He filled the glasses again and toasted the wonderful wind, then our very own mist, but the partygoers were now uneasy and soon departed to seal themselves back inside their draught-proofed dwellings.

The next day, he was gone. The doors and windows were still open, the mist still waiting outside. The woman who lived next door to him went into the kitchen and found three kelp gulls squabbling over the remains of the caviar. She felt empowered telling people he had dug a tunnel to the beach and been met by his daughter in a boat. There was no tunnel; the only sign of digging was an iris corm on the floor.

Several of the irises were gone: as far as could be ascertained from the diagram of which was where, one of every variety plus all the Blackouts, that dark velvety bloom that he'd always liked best. It was impossible to tell how long since they were taken; earth round the cavities felt hard and settled, but that could have been an effect of the mist. Many facts had changed since the arrival of our very own mist.

A psychologist said that watching television was a good family activity, that watching violence took away the desire to act violently, so domestic violence cases were now rare. Likewise, erotica and sex offences; she did not specify.

The government announced that all public holidays would be abolished, to be replaced by an annual holiday week to celebrate our very own mist and all that it had done for us, and to honour the people of the state who had shown the world how easy it was to adapt to change. Information would soon be released on the traditional rites and customs to be observed. The unions, it was reported, were fully in accord with the government; no mention of the Church.

'Mistmas proclaimed,' was the next day's headline. 'Bumper Mistmas shopping guide inside'.

Then the wind stopped.

At the elderly neighbour's house, still open as he had left it, the mist crossed the threshold and in less than a day was as dense inside as out. It would take longer in other houses but no draught excluder could keep it out.

Without the wind, walking on the beach was possible again. There seemed to be no sand left: just a bank of seaweed, about a metre high. The presence of birds was felt only when feathers grazed the face or when something moved around the foot just before it sank into the cold clammy weed. It was hard, slow progress against a mist almost solid enough to be the wall of snow it felt like. Surely not much further now, for according to the old tide tables it was high-tide time for the highest tide of the season. The weed became warmer, wetter and slippery. The mist pushed hard towards the land, then broke on the edge of the bank.

The sound of waves shocked through the frozen silence as the weed bank collapsed.

The midday sun, blinding bright, warmed but did not burn. There were no fishing boats on the silver-blue sea but on the razor-sharp horizon a tanker was proceeding towards the oil refinery. Nearer to shore there were dolphins diving for fish and, a pair of pelicans, and some silver gulls were even closer.

An idyllic scene, a dream picture, a flashback from imagined memory of another world? For is it not the familiar, the everyday, that is real? And that, surely, is our very own mist; where the irises may never bloom.

The Man in Green Goes to the Shire Council Offices

Come in, Mr Hood – I think I should call you that. We never were on familiar terms and using titles is just so pretentious these days, don't you think? I've been expecting you for a long time, a very long time. I knew you would come eventually. The lure to settle old scores…you really couldn't keep away forever.

And of course: that which you came to find and take away. Stealing. Tut tut, still the light-fingered one? Old habits die hard, as they say. You were seen entering, everyone is, on the video monitor over there. These modern devices are so efficient, I've reduced the number of my men by half, which means I've kept only those I know I can trust. You still have your, er, merry band? All well? And your good lady? Splendid! I take it you keep up with modern views on healthy diet? You're looking trim as ever yourself but one or two of your men – one in particular – well, the scourge of obesity, you know…

Forget the safe. You'd never get into it and you'd need to blast out half the wall to take it away. Besides, what you seek is in the filing cabinet over there. As I say, I knew you'd come and I felt you'd like to settle things in the time-honoured way. With a contest.

I must congratulate you on your traditional costume by the way. That green is most striking, looks quite the real thing. I've updated myself: designer leisure wear at home, but for work the humble business suit. Conveys authority without being ostentatious.

Would you care for tea or coffee? Or a glass of something stronger? Champagne is hardly appropriate but I have an excellent 2004 Shiraz. From your old estate actually. We grow vines on most of the land and converted the homestead into a boutique winery cum B&B, a most successful venture. We kept the name Lockleys Hall – it does rather impress the tourists.

One shot each. Weapon of own choice. Tradition for you of course. I understand. I'm using a modern weapon myself: an automatic. You know how firearms work? Oh dear. Well, do believe me, skill and accuracy are required, just as with your bow and arrow.

You, as my guest, will have first shot. The key to the cabinet hangs in the centre of the target. I thought you'd like that touch. You split the knot, you win the key, and the contents of the cabinet are yours to take away. No one will try to stop you, you have my guarantee as shire CEO on that.

Then it's my shot. And I will choose how and when I use it. Shall we begin…?'

Outside the Mirror

I am five minutes early. I take the lift to the second floor and cross to the School of Hairdressing. It is rather dark at the reception desk, which seems to be in front of a large black screen. There is a computer and a phone at each end of the desk, matching calculators and booking books are positioned either side of centre; but only one person is sitting there. My name is ticked off and I am directed to my right, her left, towards a black modular settee with matching armchairs on either side.

It is lighter here: a large hall, rather like a church hall, with a high ceiling and wooden floor. At the far end are four tall, narrow windows, Gothic-shaped – church hall again – but plain glass. The top section of each window is open, each exactly halfway. I can see now that the black screen behind the reception desk is actually the backs of two shelf units which face into the hall. The area seems to have been divided into identical halves: the matching shelf units screen off the reception desk, matching black modular settees and armchairs are positioned, exactly opposite, on either side. There are matching workstations on either wall, and along the non-existent centre line seven mobile workstations: double-sided mirrors above black shelves of exactly the same size as the mirrors and shelves fixed to the walls.

What kind of mind devises a place like this? And why?

The students arrive. Young. They must be young, for one cannot be an apprentice hairdresser past the age of seventeen. They all wear white tops and black trousers or skirts, but style and type of garment seem to be the wearer's choice. Some of the females wear close-fitting black jeans or leotards but the black trousers worn by male students are all loose-fitting styles and long enough, whether cuffed or not, to hang over the heels, skimming the floor. I'm a tailor: repairing frayed trouser ends is a very boring job.

An exception, a girl wearing a navy blue skirt with white polka dots, approaches. 'Hi, I'm Jill. I'm doing your hair today.' She leads me to one of the centre workstations, where we discuss how she will cut my hair. She gives me a form to sign, exonerating the school in the event of any sort of catastrophe, and goes in search of a teacher.

I look into the mirror and see, on one side, another mirror exactly the same size as the one I am looking into, but fixed to the wall. Beneath it is a rectangle of metal, not flat to the wall but slightly bowed, with conical protrusions, four across and six down, which reminds me of a Norman shield. Looking outside the mirror, I see seven shields on the wall before me and seven on the wall behind, exactly opposite each other, and seven double-sided mirrors along the exact centre of the room.

Looking back into the mirror, I can see that my chair is not precisely centred to the mirror. Will Jill lose marks for this?

Jill returns with Terry, who is tall, with spiky hair in a range of colours, and wears a shiny brown leather jacket over a long, clinging black skirt. Jill describes what she intends to do, is corrected by Terry, instructed on the cutting and shaping of the fringe, and advised to do it first while the hair is dry.

Jill picks up her scissors and we both look into the mirror. She knows that she must talk to the customer and starts with the standard question 'Are you going somewhere special tonight?'

I am good at turning questions around. Jill will not be going out tonight; I learn that she is not an apprentice, she is one of several older students doing this course full-time. This is, she says, the only hairdressing school that accepts older students, but they must pay the full fee in advance. Did she really say $20,000? When Jill finishes, two months hence, she is going to Utah with a friend and expects to work as a hairdresser during her six-month stay there. She has never worked in a salon, or anywhere else, because when she was fourteen she was injured in a car crash and has back problems. Often she aches so much that she goes to bed as soon as she gets home. Workcover is sick of paying the physio bills and has decided to pay her out next week. She will then repay her parents for this course and pay for the trip to Utah.

It is not my place to comment on inconsistencies. Besides, is there a requirement that what is said must be true? Talking to the client, gaining the client's trust, is probably part of the training. I wonder if it is recorded, then replayed, marked, criticised, but can see no sign of recording equipment.

The church hall acoustics make it hard to hear what she says; voices from the other side of the mirror seem much louder. We both look into the mirror, surveying the shape and symmetry of my fringe. Terry appears in the mirror, with another teacher who is also wearing a long, black, clinging skirt, but with a long-sleeved cream jacket of a silk-linen blend. Collarless and cuffless, it is held in at the waist by a single large button. Terry approves the fringe and I am led out of the hall into a side chapel to have my hair shampooed.

The floorboards, once highly varnished, are still shiny enough to reflect shapes and shadows but expansion/contraction has caused the varnish over the grooves to crack. Trying to sweep across the boards would be frustrating, broom hairs catching in the grooves. The smarter operator sweeps along the boards, then uses dustpan and brush to gather up the hair and put it into one of the twin bins on either side of twin shelf units. Similarly, pushing trolleys of equipment is easier along than across the boards. The teachers could use this as a test to identify the brighter pupils.

Afraid of slipping, I walk carefully.

When we return to the workstation, Jill goes very carefully through the routine for seating the customer, exactly centre. While she positions the equipment trolley, I look into my mirror and see the teacher in the cream jacket talking to an older man whose grey hair looks like a hairpiece. They are in front of a workstation on the wall behind but I hear her clearly.

'It's good to see you here on the floor.' There is a blend of affection and respect in her voice.

He is a person of some importance: the director, or, perhaps, the designer of the floor.

Next to me, a young woman is having colour applied to her hair. The top section has been painted in the colour the fabric industry calls shiraz, and now one of the sides is being painted indigo. The operator is painting it with a three-centimetre brush, slowly, carefully, almost strand by strand; occasionally he puts down the indigo brush and adds more of the shiraz colour to the hair piled on top of the woman's head.

I see all this in her mirror. If I look into my mirror, I see my face and the top of Jill's head as, bent over – surely this is not good for the back – she works on the hair at the back of my head. I cannot see what she is doing and she is concentrating so hard that she has, thank goodness, forgotten that she is supposed to talk to the client.

I watch the painting again, and listen to the conversion between the woman and the operator. He is very tall, medium build, of dark complexion, and wearing the uniform white T-shirt and black trousers. His name is Romeo; he does not look Italian. Romeo is worried because he will be thirty on Saturday, rather old to start in hairdressing. He used to own a restaurant but his ageing parents are finding it too hard, the hours too long, so he sold it and that was how he paid for the hairdressing course. He is Australian, born three years after his parents came here from Lebanon. He supposes they thought Romeo a good name for their first child born in Australia. 'But I wasn't too happy with what they called my sister Juliet. That was awful at school!'

'Was the restaurant Lebanese?'

'Oh no, takeaway: fish and chips, hamburgers…but I knew my customers really well, what they wanted, they didn't have to tell me… Ah, I've run out of product, I'll get more. Would you like a coffee? Tea? Springwater?'

She would not.

'Product' is generic for anything that is applied to the hair.

He moves to the side of the mirror, disappears, then reappears in my mirror. Jill stands up and they hug.

He says to me, 'Hi. I'm Romeo. Do you come here often?'

This is my first time. But I say nothing.

As though I have answered, he says, 'That's good.'

He and Jill have a conversation about girls in the IVF program or trying to get into it. Juliet has just got in; good news, she can get married now. They agree that it seems impossible these days for anyone to get pregnant without IVF: it's the pollution, the exhaust fumes, chemicals in the food… In my mirror, I watch them nod knowingly.

Romeo becomes aware that the customer is being neglected and says, 'Was it like that in your day?'

Oh, Romeo! Minus marks!

'No, quite the opposite. Having children you didn't want was the problem.'

They look puzzled.

'Wouldn't you just have an abortion, then?'

'No. That was illegal.'

They stare, disbelieving.

'If a girl who was not married had a baby, that was shameful. The babies were usually adopted by people who could not have children.'

'You mean people actually took other people's children!'

Total scepticism: I am telling them fairy stories, or, most likely, I have Alzheimers. They cannot believe me; I cannot believe their unbelief.

Romeo goes off in search of product. Jill takes some hair from the right side of my head and draws it between two fingers in such a way that the hair where the fingers taper is longer than the hair near the hand; she surveys it critically, then trims away the longer hair.

Looking ahead, I see an elderly woman drinking coffee or tea. This is reflected in the mirror in front of her; I can see both her face and the back of her head, which is wrapped in a towel. Still looking ahead, but outside the mirror, I can see a young man being shown, in a hand-held mirror, how the back of his hair has been cut. He seems pleased. A small-waisted, large-bosomed girl wearing a black four-tiered skirt and a white lace blouse over a white, tight tank top walks in front of me, removes the towel from the elderly woman's head and starts putting large rollers into her hair. The grey-haired man walks in front of me; he is obviously making comments to the operator, whom I cannot see, about the young man's haircut. He steps, lightly, like a dancer, to the centre, and disappears. A few minutes later, he walks in front of me again, and hugs the girl in the white lace blouse.

Romeo returns with product, and his teacher, who is shorter and slighter than Romeo, and wearing trousers so long that the cuffs drag across the floor. I hear the teacher introduced – another Terry – but no more, because someone on the other side starts using a hair dryer.

Jill takes some hair from the left side of my head and draws it between two fingers in such a way that the hair where the fingers taper is longer than the hair near the hand; she surveys it critically, then trims away the longer hair.

Anyone who appears and disappears must be on my side of the mirror, behind me: a reflection. Anyone who appears, disappears and reappears is behind the mirror, in front of me: a real person. It's like watching a ballet: constant movement of the black and white clad dancers, real or reflected, moving in and out of my field of vision. Sometimes I glimpse the grey-haired man, the star dancer, perhaps the choreographer. Echoing voices and hair dryers provide the soundtrack.

Meanwhile, Jill, reflected yet tangible, is snipping and trimming, left, right, centre, never satisfied, seeking perfect symmetry, so a little more off, here, there…

At last, her teacher appears and tells her to dry the hair with a diffuser. My hair is already dry so before Jill can dry it she must spray it with water, but the spray bottle is empty so she takes it away to refill it. Terry makes a parting comment that the colour is good. An interesting comment: my hair has not been coloured. I have been here for two hours just having it cut. Coming here will cost half as much in dollars, but more than twice as much in time. Retired, I now have more time than dollars, just one of the changes I must accept. The saying 'time is money' is still true, but the words have changed sides

Half an hour later, my hair has been misted, moussed and diffused. Jill goes to find Terry for final judgement. I must pretend to be pleased, though I have no real interest: hair grows, becomes a nuisance, needs cutting. So I look. The fair – but never blonde – hair that does not show grey has been neatly cut. Surely, after all Jill's care, it cannot be longer on one side! No, it is the face, the ageing, jowly face that has sagged. I study the coarse-featured face on the large head. Bad skin: grainy, pasty; the complexion of years of working indoors. The nose and mouth are large, though in proportion for the size of the head; the eyes seem small because the skin beneath is bulbous, the wrinkled lids hang low. There are deep lines across the forehead but the slightly puffy cheeks are almost smooth. The expression is half vacant, half petulant, showing a life of no real achievement, too insipid even to be called wasted.

It is an oppressive sight. I do not want it to be me. I could – should – move and see, outside the mirror, a new past in a face from the other side…

The rumble of thunder reminds me of my mother covering all the mirrors with black cloth because a mirror broken by reflected lightning would bring seven times seven years' bad luck.

There are too many mirrors here. It is too late.

The Stone-gatherer

He was there again this morning, as I knew he would be. Every three or four years, there is a week of unusually violent winter storms and then, at low tide on the first calm day, he will be there collecting stones. Every day for a week, sometimes two, and then he goes.

I used to tell myself that he surely could not come again: to a child, he seemed ancient with his long grey hair held in a ponytail with a strip of brown cloth, and the slow, deliberate movements of an old man moving along the beach selecting, collecting. The stones he took were always large, large smooth ovals of one colour all over, never striated, never black.

'The black ones are the guardians of this beach. You must never take them away.'

'What about the others? Where do you take them?

'Oh, back to the Shadowland and then on a long voyage to the half-moon so that dead souls can be released.'

It was a good enough story for a child. When I, the daughter of geologists, tried to tell him about rocks and the beach and erosion, he shook his head and laughed as if my facts were just stories.

When I was fourteen, he picked up a pink stone of a size to fill the palm of my hand and said, 'This one is yours, but you must not take it away. It must stay here and grow until it is time for me to gather it.'

That was the year I wanted to be his helper, to become the next stone-gatherer, but every one that I picked up was rejected, put gently down again on the sand, though I could not see any difference between mine and the ones that he took.

'Girls never can find the right ones. They lack the power to discriminate,' he said, putting a large yellow oval into his denim bag.

That hurt. And shocked, I had not met such an attitude. I followed him that day when he left the beach, but he saw me and turned back.

'That was a mistake,' he said. 'Now you will not see me again.'

He was, indeed, not there the next day but I told myself it was time for him to go, that he would not have been there anyway, though it was only the fourth day. I found the pink stone and took it home; I took some guardian stones too, but dropped those along the path. I had to show him he was wrong.

When I reached home, I was greeted by angry parents. They lectured me on the foolishness of speaking to strangers, and on betrayal of the trust they had placed in me: for the rest of that summer I was not to go to the beach by myself. It didn't matter. I was content to stay in my room drawing pictures of the beach, of stones, and of the stone-gatherer on his journey to the half-moon; those last I hid.

Time was set aside most days by one of my parents, sometimes both, to take me to the beach. Always they talked about tides and rocks, how the sand would have gone in forty, perhaps thirty, years because steps that could be taken to prevent erosion were being blocked by a group of crusading Greenies who believed that nature should be allowed to take its course.

Once only, my father mentioned him. 'It was kind of you to speak to that poor man. He's a very lonely person – a tortured soul – probably harmless, but you can never be sure, especially at your age.'

'Why is he a tortured soul?'

'His wife and baby daughter were drowned fifteen years ago. People here thought he'd killed them, some still do think that, but it was proved in court that he was nowhere near at the time. It was one of those terrible accidents that sometimes happen. He had a breakdown afterwards and was in hospital for a long time. He still has periods in hospital now, one of the reasons people are so afraid of him. Except you. We don't want you to be frightened of people but it was very silly to speak to a stranger like that. At your age, you lack the ability to discriminate. If you like to help people, you'd better train to be a counsellor.'

Three years later, I was away, studying law, and did not come back here until I retired. I checked on the case of course, and it was as my father had told me. What shocked me was to read that they had drowned in their own swimming pool on a hot summer afternoon. I had assumed they were drowned in the sea, had dreamt of their faces in the water that lapped the rocks at high tide, always at night with a half-moon lighting a path across the sea and the stone-gatherer on that path, trying to reach them. I checked newspaper reports, to find that the wraithlike, long-haired blonde of my dream was a stocky redhead with short-cropped hair. She was a medal-winning swimmer, and qualified lifesaver, hence the initial suspicion surrounding her death. It was deduced, from the medical evidence, that the baby had fallen into the deepest part of the Olympic-size pool and, one to two hours later, the mother, too distraught to act rationally, had drowned trying to save the child. When the pool was drained, some smooth pink stones were found there; friends of the couple – the devoted, happy couple – said that he would bring stones from the beach for the child and put them around the side of the pool. Speculation was that the gate had been left unlocked and the child had crawled after the stones, knocked them into the pool, then fallen in after them. One of those terrible accidents…but there are no accidents, there is always human error.

When I returned, a judge, and under sentence of death myself, I took a house overlooking the beach, a beach devastated by the storms of the intervening years. The sand had gone, as my parents had foretold, and the steps down to the beach had been completely destroyed. It was a hard climb for me, but I wanted to return the pink stone, which had neither grown, nor shrunk. The climb up was even harder. I wondered how the stone-gatherer would manage. Apparently with ease, though it was another year before he came.

I had enquiries made, and learned that he takes the stones back to his house and arranges them in the pool to make a picture, the same picture through each layer: the first was a Celtic cross, the second a Buddhist mandala. When the pool is full, he sits there for a night, seemingly in prayer, then, carefully, reverently, starts removing the stones. Pink ones are taken to the cemetery and placed on the grave of his daughter; the rest are taken to the causeway on the other side of the point, where once there was a lighthouse. Some of them would be taken back by the tides to the beaches where he first found them. Maybe he knows this.

He works until there are only seven smooth stones left in the deepest part of the pool. These are never moved: seeing them, he will stand on the edge of the pool and howl. A desperate, desolate sound that terrifies his neighbours, who make calls, have him taken to hospital. These neighbours claim that the outbursts occurred at the time of a full moon. I checked. It was not so, nor was it half-moon.

When he leaves the hospital, he returns to the coves and beaches round the point, gathering for another picture. The one he is building now is the profile of a judge, in robes and wig, looking down at a half-moon of pink stones in the corner of the pool. One hand is shown, holding the black cap once used for sentencing to death. When I saw it, seven months ago, the pool was not quite half full. It will be the last picture, if he lives long enough to complete it. I know that I shall not see it.

I saw him yesterday, from my window, as he made his way down. He looked a little older: the long hair, still in a ponytail, is now white and he is thinner, the bones more obvious. He still carries a denim bag, surely another, though it looks exactly the same. Once on the beach, he turned the other way so did not see my pink stone but he will find it today, or tomorrow, and gather it. I do not hope for a miracle cure. I am the rationalist child of my parents. It is just the sentimentalist quirk to which the dying are entitled that I want him to gather the pink stone he once allotted to me and give it a place in the final picture.